Copyright © 2023 Anna Elizabeth Judd
All Rights Reserved.

Paperback ISBN: 9781648731211

Hardcover ISBN: 9781648731846

EBOOK ISBN: 9781648731228

Printed in the United States of America

Published by:
Writer's Publishing House
Prescott, AZ 86301

Design Project Management and Book Launch
by Writers Publishing House

The Hourglass of el Diablo

by *Anna Elizabeth Judd*

Writer's Publishing House

Preface

"Anyone who raises himself up will be humbled, and anyone who humbles himself will be raised up."

Matthew 23: 1

In the Old West, during a time when the terrain was hostile, lived a man named Jed. His father alone raised him 'till he was a young teen. Jed escapes the brutal acts of an abusive parent and befriends the devil himself. From there, his escapades carry them across the countryside, wreaking havoc on every unsuspecting victim that crosses their paths. Then one day, the evil tactics of his friend, Diablo, cause his blurred vision to clear, leaving a scared man alone in the desert, wondering where to find answers to the questions he seeks to le

Appearing Desolate

The days appear to be desolate now, with only the vacant sight of cacti and sand. Time lost its meaning, it seemed to span forever without any acknowledgment of my existence. I spent days wandering through the desert looking for a way out of the wilderness, only the end never came.

I am going to start this story from the end, where maybe the answer to my fate will become clear at the beginning. Not too long ago, I buried the one being in my life I ever loved. Our spirits met when I was just a young boy who had the world at my fingertips.

Raised as a rancher's son looking after cattle and horses, I learned the value of a hard day's work. My father was a hardened man who did not know the meaning of love. I took the beatings as they came and went, like the wind that blows through the trees. Eventually, they just became a part of everyday life.

One day a miracle happened: we had an old mare that pulled my father's buckboard for many years until she got too old, and then he kept her for breeding. She gave birth to a colt in the field one night and because of her age, the birth of such a large foal got the best of her and she perished during the birth, which meant the colt was an orphan; my father in all his wisdom wanted to shoot the foal. But I begged him to let me raise the colt.

I milked the cows and fed him for many months until he was old enough to graze on his own. We became inseparable; for the first time in my life, I found out what it meant to love something.

I worked on the farm during the days 'til my fingers bled, and tended to my colt in the evenings, which is when I learned to escape the reality of my life. It was the only time I ever felt free from the clutches of my father's anger.

One night while watching the colt, I had not been able to come up with a name and knew I had to choose one soon. While I cleaned the straw out of the barn, he stood staring at me, and I noticed the blaze on his face. It looked like an hourglass and fit him perfectly. He was the only thing in my life that became a symbol of truth, and the one happy presence that could stand my company. I turned into the one thing I hated the most: my father. The years passed and time stood for nothing; there was no end to the path I walked, evil and wickedness poured from every fiber of my being.

I woke up one morning and found myself in this wasteland of despair. The only thing I could see for miles was the body of my horse lying dead in the sand. I had no memory of the previous events that led to this catastrophe. I was faced with the daunting task of walking in a desert. I started to gather my meager belongings from the saddlebags when I noticed something lying on the sand next to the body of my horse. As I reached down to grab the shiny object glistening in the sunlight, the rays blocked my vision, until I shadowed the item close to my chest. The sweltering heat, however, heated the metal and it burned the palm of my hand. As it fell, a memory flooded my mind. It was something I placed in my saddlebags a year ago and forgotten about until now. The item brought images of sitting in the chair next to my mother's bed, watching the life drain from her body, hating God.

In her last minutes of breath, she handed me two things I never wanted to see again: a cross and Bible. How could a loving God snatch a boy's mother and leave him in the clutches of the horrid man he called father?

"Look, the day of God is coming, when the spoils taken
from you will be shared among you." **Zechariah 14**

Moments in Time

The morning after Mom died went like any other with my father. He just got up, went to the stove, poured what little coffee was left in the pot, sat down at the table, and stared at the wall while he sipped from the cup. Not a word was uttered from his mouth for more than three days. So naturally, I did my best to stay out of his way.

After dinner the next evening my father slipped on his coat and walked out the door, leaving me alone. I waited up 'till early morning, but my eyes grew heavy. I wondered if he'd ever return. The innocence of youth spared me the knowledge of his escapades for a short time.

I laid in my bed waiting to hear the rooster's crow, but then I heard sounds that brought me to my feet, noises that could only come from a woman's voice. I ran into the kitchen, just knowing it was Mom. She had come back! But my enthusiastic pace halted at the sight of an unfamiliar scene.

A woman was standing in the kitchen, I had never seen before, cooking at the stove that was my mother's.

In a rage, I hollered, "Who are you? And what are you doing at Mom's stove?"

My outburst was promptly met by the backside of my father's hand. He demanded I show respect to my new mother.

"New mother?" I said. "She is not my mother and never will be."

"Boy!" he demanded. "You will show manners, or else."

Obliging his request, I calmly proceeded to the door and made my way to the barn— the one place I found peace. Hourglass became a great sounding board; he listened and did not hit or judge me.

The time flew by each day, as one merged into another, before long I could not tell the difference. My father would bring home a new woman every night, and she' be standing at the stove, cooking some meal for us. I learned to sit and eat without saying a word. Some of the women would occasionally ask my name or if I needed anything.

Then as fate would have it, the night came that destroyed any youth I may have had left. An urge from nature called for a trip to the outhouse, but as I entered the kitchen my father was standing behind a woman bent over the table.

Since neither one noticed my presence, I ended up watching the happenings for a bit. The images that I witnessed that night remained in my mind and gradually developed into a hatred for women. As a young man, completely ignorant and wanting answers, I made my way to town the next morning.

The behavior I witnessed changed my personality overnight; I became determined to re-create my father's activities no matter the cost to my well-being. An unrelenting rage came over my soul that grew with the light of each day; it was almost as if I carried another presence in my body.

Since I grew up in this small town, my father's escapades were the talk of the town. So, my reason for wanting to leave home was understood. The only option at my age was the local livery stable. As a friend of my family the owner gave me a job in the evenings after my home chores. It opened the door to endless possibilities. It gave me the financial means to initiate the encounters I sought. A young man with money and drive could get whatever they wanted.

One evening while I was left alone to attend to the livery stable, a man of unknown origin came in wanting a bed and stall for his horse. I remember he was tall and thin, wearing a long dark duster and two sidearms. It was usual to see someone carrying dual pistols. So being a nosy kid, I asked the man why he carried two sidearms. Although, he never answered my question, his response stayed with me forever.

The man flipped a large gold coin in his hand. I remember how it glistened in the faint lighting. He offered it to me as a tip if I would take his saddlebags to the marshal's office for the night and have them back at the livery stable at dawn. The tip was more than I would make in six months mucking stalls for this old man. I gladly took the money and attended to his request; however, this task led the way to my inevitable ending.

I learned at a much later date that the man in black was one of the most notorious gunfighters in the west, for which many people sought revenge. As a prodigy of my father, doing a competent job was expected, therefore his belongings were returned at dawn as requested. I had not only befriended the devil himself but forsaken my soul. Of which Diablo held in the palm of his hand, ready to squash in the event I failed a task. Although, his demands were not without payment, and the reimbursements of wealth and riches were beyond my wildest dreams. And his unyielding plan worked perfectly. I would never again worry about the daunting tasks of life, such as mucking stalls or tending to farm animals for a man who beat me in the blink of an eye.

My walk home each night served to gather strength from the rage building inside. On the few instances I asked for a ride, my father boldly stated that the task built character. In reality, he did not trust me to use the buckboard.

As time passed, my new friend worked to fill my head with reasons to combat my father's wrath. The ideas rolled around like a cow chewing her cud; coupled with the added time walking home, my fury built into a fevered rage. I was anxious for him to engage me with one of his rampages. Therefore, by the time I reached the house, my body ached for an altercation. However, the yearning would never be satisfied. As I reached for the knob, my hands trembled. *Would the anger be enough to overpower the man I hated?* I paused for a moment to contemplate my decision.

I took a deep breath and turned the doorknob. The hatred raged, but the scene left me standing in the middle of the room, stupefied. My eyes scanned the house for some remnant of life. *What?* The walls were empty, dishes removed, boots stacked in the corner were gone, along with all the furniture. It was all gone…. every portion of his existence vanished.

As I searched for a note, a flash of fear came over my soul. I darted out of the house in a fit of rage. My only true vision of hope remained in the barn. My mind raced, praying he left the one shining light in my life. Again, as I reached the barn, my heart pounded. I panicked until a faint sound filtered through the air. In the corner, I saw movement in the rays of moonlight shining through the door. It was Hourglass standing in a pile of hay, quiet and unharmed. The relief that overtook my mind was incredible; maybe my father had a smidgen of love left in his soul. Nonetheless, I promised to vanquish all memory of him forever. No matter what, to me, my father died that day.

"Do not stifle the Spirit or despise the gift of prophecy with contempt; test everything and hold on to what is good and shun every form of evil."

Thessalonians 19

The Encounter

When I saw that Hourglass was safely tucked away in the barn, the rage somehow calmed when I entered the house and realized for the first time, I was alone in this place. As my amazement grew over the idea of being alone, I made my way through the house, littering parts of my attire across the room. My boots hit the floor in the living room and my hat fell in the bedroom. It was surprising to still see my bed against the wall in my bedroom. Suddenly, it was the most comfortable mattress I'd even slept on. Not that I had laid on many other beds but this one, it was just the point of being alone without the fear of my father's hatred for his only son.

This is when the voice of vengeance took over every pore of my body and soul— nothing would ever stop me from settling the score with my father. It was the night I left the one thing behind that could save my soul: peace.

Since the chickens were gone, there was no alarm clock, so my morning did not start 'til mid-afternoon the next day— another pleasure I quickly learned to like. Still haunted by the lashings from my father, fear lingered, bringing me to my feet expecting the usual wallop. Instead, I was greeted by a welcome sight waiting outside the front door. In my haste to come inside last night, I forgot to latch the barn doors, so Hourglass made his way to the house.

The joy quickly filled my body; the one thing I loved had come to find me. He pushed on my chest with his nose, and I stood on the porch patting Hourglass on the forehead. My giggles felt right, just to spite my father for having a horse standing on the porch. Once our greetings were over, the afternoon sun settled low on the horizon, so I decided to fetch some dinner in town. Since money was no issue, due to my current employment, I took Hourglass by the jaw and led him to the barn, closed the doors to keep him safe, and began my trip to find supper.

The monotony of the road to town left my mind wandering in all sorts of directions, mostly about how I was going to spend my newly found wealth. I was able to buy the items on display instead of just looking at them, a concept I had never known. The relief I'd been seeking smacked me square in the face; escaping the clutches of my father felt good. But my ignorance left me temporarily innocent.

I'd never entered town in the early evening, which was a novel event. In the past, I would have been doing chores while my father meandered about, fiddling as he pleased. The townsmen were lighting the lanterns and Main Street was coming to life. I heard the piano player in the saloon tapping away on some tune, girls in fancy dresses being swung around by cowboys needing to have fun, shots of whiskey sitting on the bar waiting, people coming out of the restaurant after eating supper, and the stage dropping off passengers for the last time today.

After taking in all the sights of the township, I did not know where to begin, so I figured the first stop must be supper. Then maybe, a new set of duds, and of course, a new saddle and tack for Hourglass. I was a big man in town and people needed to pay attention.

Dinner options were limited since the only restaurant with style and class was in the hotel lobby. This eatery had the best of everything on the menu; however, the only item that interested me was the Porterhouse steak. It was served with green beans, baked potato, and freshly baked bread; a meal never tasted so good. The rich, full flavor of the steak melted in my mouth, smothered with sautéed mushrooms and onions, which only served to enhance the experience. These comforts only expedited my drive to serve Diablo and continue my life of luxury. The waitress returned to inquire about my dinner and asked if it was satisfactory.

My only response to the question was pulling the large roll of money from my pocket and placing a tip that totaled more than she'd make in a month. Her dumfounded look stayed static while I strolled out the door and meandered on my way.

As I strolled down the boardwalk, lost in my reveling, the owner of the mercantile was turning the "open" sign to "closed." I noticed the movement out of the corner of my eye and rushed to the entrance.

"Wait, I need some new clothes, and I'll make it worth your while," I hollered.

The storekeeper paused and stated, "Alright, come on, but hurry up."

Since I passed the shop each night, there was no need to look at anything, I already knew what I wanted: the most expensive jeans, boots, hat, shirt, vest, and belt in the place. Once I convinced the shop owner my money was not stolen or borrowed from an unwilling townsman, he sold me my goods, and let me be on my way. The only difference was the man who emerged from the mercantile this time wore a veil of malevolence.

I carried my newfound authority down the boardwalk to the livery stable. It was curious to watch people give me a wide berth as they walked past. *The experience was exhilarating.*

The young man that was hired to replace me was working late when I paid to have my saddle ready in the morning. I was the big man in town now and wanted to announce my prowess. After which, I had the night to myself, no one to bother me or make demands of my time. *Wow! This was an incredible feeling. All I need is another job with my new friend.*

As fate would have it, someone grabbed my arm and drew me into the alley.

"Hey," I stated. Then when I looked up in the dimly lit alley, and noticed the silhouette of my friend's face, "What do I call you? We have talked many times and I don't know your name."

In a calm, almost eerie voice, "El Diablo, or just Diablo, whichever you prefer."

The tone in his voice sent shivers up my spine, and I questioned my decision for a brief second. In my young mind, the idea of money overshadowed morality. It would be the last time any thread of conscience passed through my body— the trap had been set and there was no turning back.

The next job sent me to the marshal's office with another package. But the package was different this time; I was to deliver it to the marshal's office instead of picking one up.

Diablo cautiously handed me the package, explaining once again the importance of my job. "Oh!" he said, "Don't forget to make sure the marshal sees your new duds and how classy you look."

I took the compliment very serious, as someone noticed my presence. Diablo's words turned my slow uncertain pace into an arrogant stroll across the street into the marshal's office. When I entered, he was seated behind the desk busy filling out paperwork. When he looked up, a flash of surprise overtook his face.

His attitude was annoying. "Marshal, I need you to hold this package for safekeeping."

"Where did you get this from? Aren't you Jacob's son Jed?"

"Yeah, that's me," I stated in a cocky voice.

"Where did this come from?" he stated again. My affiliation with Diablo had brought my rage to a head and I would let no one talk to me that way anymore. So, I refused to tell him.

"I'm going to ask you one more time, where did you get this package? And now that I take a look at you, where did you get those clothes? You don't have the money for that kind of stuff."

"It's none of your business, and yes I do!" I told him.

The marshal was disgusted with my attitude and chased me out of the office. "I better not get any word of thefts in town, or I am coming after you!"

I ignored the babble and proceeded to meet up with Diablo. The idea of the contents in that package never crossed my mind until it was too late. My vision was blurred by greed, which was the only thing that drove my existence for years. It did not matter who got hurt, killed, stepped on, or run over, as long as we got our just desserts.

Diablo was waiting for me on the porch, "What took you so long? Did you have any trouble with the marshal?"

"No, man, I took care of that marshal, did not tell him a thing. Don't worry, I can handle myself," I stated.

"Good…. meet me tomorrow at the old mill on the south road out-of-town, ten o'clock," he told me. "Don't be late!"

"Umm, okay, but I don't have a horse to ride yet."

"Well, you better get that nag in the barn rode then," he yelled as he disappeared into the woods. His comment fueled the fire. I'd show him what a good horse Hourglass was, and he'd regret calling him a nag.

It had been almost a day and a half since I'd been home, so my priority was getting Hourglass some water and feed. Not to mention, my lack of sleep. My eyelids were starting to feel like miniature weights and my head was spinning. The only thing I wanted at the moment was to take care of Hourglass and get some sleep. My bed was still in the house, but spending too much time in that empty house gave me the chills. So, I decided to take Hourglass down the creek. The water was crystal clear, and the grass grew knee-high around the banks. It was a perfect place to get some peace for a while.

I settled down on the ground and leaned against the old oak tree next to the creek. It had been there since my dad was a kid. I'd spent many days down here sleeping next to the stream, escaping my father's wrath. The bubbling currents were soothing. After Hourglass settled in grazing, the steady hum of the water flowing down the creek put me right to sleep. However, my slumber was interrupted when someone kicked the sole of my boot, demanding I wake up and answer some questions. "What? Who are you?" I shouted.

"Do you know a man that goes by Diablo?" he said sternly.

I stated again, "Who are you? What are you doing on my property?"

"My name is not important right now, where is your father or the owner of this land?"

"My father is dead, and I own this place. Now, what do you want here?" I tried to buy time while I could think of some response to his questions. "I don't know any such a man."

"You were seen in town delivering a package from him to the marshal last night. So, you better come clean, boy," the man said.

Playing along with his dumb kid comment, I stated, "Hey, I'm just trying to get by, a guy offered me a few bucks to deliver some package. I did not ask his name and don't remember what he looked like."

The answer seemed to satisfy the man, and he left without any more questions. However, the encounter left me a bit shaky. There was no doubt in my mind now that Diablo wore many hats.

"There is need for shrewdness here: anyone clever may interpret the number of the beast: it is a number of a human being, the number 666."

Revelation 12: 18

Time Passes

After being jolted awake from my restful slumber, it looked like the time had come to make Hourglass a riding horse. I grabbed his jaw again and led him back to the barn to a small pen we'd built for breaking colts. The hardest part was already finished since I had handled him from a young foal.

I began the process by placing a halter on his head, along with a long rope attached for me to grab and hold onto when I finally mounted him for the first time. Young horses don't take to a bit in their mouth at first, so a rope halter and line are enough to get them started.

The first step to breaking a colt is sacking them out with a blanket. It gets them use to something being laid on their back and touching their body. Once they can accept the blanket, it's time for the saddle and cinch around their girth.

Most young horses who are trained this way don't buck, so on occasion, when one does, it makes a man know he's alive. Hourglass took to the blanket very well; he only had a little white in his eye showing. The saddle would be a different story, I was sure. I went into the barn and got the old saddle that we used on the young horses the first time; it saved the good ones from getting beat up or damaged.

As I reached the gate, Hourglass was right there following close behind, I guess not wanting to be left alone. I let him continue on his course. Once we were all the way into the barn, we went back to the small pen; he never faltered. This was the first time I had ever had a horse react in this manner, but I guess raising him as his mother gave me some advantage, and believe me, I used this to my benefit.

Once back in the round pen, I grabbed the old saddle and threw it up on his back. Hourglass had grown very tall, so it was a stretch for me to reach that high. However, he got used to the stirrups hitting his sides, plus the cinch tightening around his girth. If a young horse is going to falter, this is the time. A cinch tightened around their girth is restricting, which makes them feel vulnerable. Hourglass took the ordeal with great confidence. Once he settled with the cinch snug, I pushed him around the pen so he could get comfortable with the saddle on his back. At first, he seemed punchy but then it was like old times. I stepped back, he turned and walked right over to me, ready for my next command. *What a relief!* Since this was my first time training a horse alone.

Once he settled in the center with me, I took the rope in my left hand and swung into the saddle. I was expected a fight but to my surprise, he just stood quiet, never flinching.

I took a moment and patted him on the neck, saying, "Good boy, I am not going to hurt you." Flabbergasted at his response, I continued with the training and guessed I'd quit when and if a problem occurred.

"Okay then, Hourglass. Let's ride." I told him.

I took a deep breath when I threw my new saddle upon his back, hoping he would not decide to use this time and cut loose. Yet, nothing; he did nothing.

"Alright then, I'll get the bridle and away we go," I told him again.

Just like clockwork, he took the bit with ease, only a little chomping at first. *Well here goes nothing.* I put my foot in the stirrup and took a deep breath, I could feel my heart pounding and my hands shaking. The horse training my father knew was to beat them into submission. I wanted to take a softer approach.

Once in a while, a broncobuster would come by the ranch asking my father for work and he'd have them train the young colts. Many years ago, one of the men was Indian and I learned a lot from him. He allowed me to sit quietly on the pasture fence and watch.

I sat down in the saddle and put my foot in the stirrup to be safe. I let him settle for a few minutes. Then nudged his sides asking him to move, and a gradual hump developed in the middle of his back. I knew the rodeo was about to begin. He took three steps, and we were flying high; oh, that horse could buck when he got the urge.

We made our way around the pen several times until he decided I was not coming off and gave up. It was the most exhilaration I'd ever felt. Since he settled right down, I figured it was a good time to get the handling done. I hopped off and opened the gate. In a moment's notice, we were down the road as fast as Hourglass would go.

"Yahoo!!!" I hollered. "Let's go, buddy."

After he had worked up a good sweat on his neck, I slowed him up and we walked back to the house. The summer air was so thick you could have cut it with a knife. No wonder Hourglass worked up such a sweat. I'd for sure have to give him a good brushing tonight.

By the time I was done in the barn, the evening had turned into night, and only the shimmering highlights from the moon shone through the trees. I was ready for some shuteye after the last few days. But, as I headed for the house, I noticed an alluring vision standing on the porch. My pace came to a screeching halt when the reflection of her bosom illuminated in the moonlight. She was exquisite… the glittery red material wrapped around her perfectly curvy body.

It was a surprise. She left me paralyzed at the porch step; her eyes twinkled with the anticipation of my presence. As the daze obscuring my vision cleared, I could see her gleaming smile, her tantalizing presence was my second exhilaration for the day. She just smiled with the sweetness of a Sunday morning cinnamon roll fresh out of the oven.

"Hello," she said. "Do you remember me?"

"Oh yeah, the restaurant," I said.

"Well, I could not stop thinking about your invitation to come to visit. Do you remember?"

"Hell, yeah, I remember, darlin! Glad you came by; I'm leaving town tomorrow. I may not be back in these parts for a long time, maybe never. I hope you didn't have your heart set on some long-term relationship?"

"Uh, well, I was not ruling that out. Are you all all right? You seem different."

"Nope the same guy, why?"

"I thought you were a nice guy and wanted to come and get to know you better."

"Well, you can get to know me for a night?"

Maybe I should just go? I'm sorry to have bothered you." The evil rage gradually consumed my soul.

"No, no…. I'm sorry; you just caught me off guard. Please stay. Come on inside. Oh, please don't be alarmed; the house is very empty."

I opened the door to let her inside, "Oh my, what happened? Did someone rob you?"

"No, I wish that was all. It's a long story, but this is my father's ranch, and he left a short time ago. I came back from my job at the livery stable to find everything including him gone. After my mother died, I guess he wanted to leave. One night in the livery stable, a man came in looking to board his horse and offered me a job. We are heading out in the morning, and I have no idea if we'll ever get back in these parts again."

She was right; my attitude had changed drastically. To this day, I can't for the life of me figure out why she stayed that night. Maybe she saw something, a glimmer of good trapped inside the evil that was emerging. The memory would hold my thoughts hostage for many years to come. On the long, lonely nights, this image kept a small part of me sane; it seemed to be my one single attachment to the past.

I can remember how our eyes met with the intensity of a bull defending his territory, fixed on holding his position. I drew her in close with my hand on her lower back. She responded with a flip of my hat, causing us to succumb to our cravings of the night.

The night hours faded, and I found myself hating the sweet woman who shared my bed. In the light of day, the sight of her disgusted me. My feet hit the floor in a rage as I picked up her clothes and threw them on the porch, shouting for her to get out of my sight.

The startling change in my demeanor left her shaking in fear as she snuck out the door. I watched her struggling to get dressed on the front porch before I went scavenging for food in the house. Diablo would be here soon and something inside me knew she must be gone before he showed up; I feared for her safety. When she was finally out of sight, I took a deep breath, grabbed some food, and headed for the barn. Hourglass was waiting for some breakfast as well. I tossed him what was left of the hay and headed for the house one last time.

A sense of sadness filled my soul as I shoved my clothes and belongings into the saddlebags. I dug through my hidden compartment in the closet and grabbed two precious items; the only remnants of my mother and placed them in the bottom of the saddlebags.

As I made my way out of the house, a vision of my mother appeared in the rocking chair on the porch. She was swaddling a small infant, singing "Rock-a-bye Baby." The sound of her beautiful voice was deafening. I winced in pain over the image. For a moment, I longed to be that baby again and remain protected by my mother's love.

But suddenly, the sweet vision was interrupted by a vision of my father standing over her grave yelling, "It should be you in that coffin instead of her." His words pierced my soul. "Get out of here; stop sobbing and git them chores done."

The horrifying vision brought me to my senses, and I tucked any emotions away so deep no one would ever hurt me again. *Oh…. God!* I blurted out. I realized how much time had passed with my dallying; Diablo would be waiting, and he was not a patient man.

I grabbed my stuff and headed for the barn. It was a fast-saddling session in history; Hourglass would have to deal with the situation. It surprised me that he took every step in stride, and we kicked it into high gear. By the time I reached the meeting spot, my horse was covered in sweat and needed a spell to rest. So, when we arrived and Diablo was not in sight, it was a blessing in disguise. However, it was odd because he was never late and always demanded promptness.

Once I realized we beat Diablo to the meeting place, it gave me time to grab my canteen and give Hourglass some water while we waited. We waited for almost an hour before he showed up, then from out of nowhere he appeared. It was eerie, he could just vanish in a split second. As usual, he wore his long dark duster, that just happened to cover his inner darkness. Although, I would learn that was normal, and for a while, I found the image appealing. However, today he had a demeanor that shook my soul. "You need to follow me, without question…. do you understand?"

I nodded, "Yes."

"Good," then he ambled back to his horse.

We headed into a section of the woods that was completely unfamiliar, which was odd since I grew up in these parts. My father had worked at the lumber mill for many years. Me and my surrogate brother played around here but never found this section of woods. It was somewhat unnerving; the trees were so thick the light almost vanished completely. We walked for quite a while, leading the horses because it was dangerous riding in woods this thick. Then all of a sudden, it opened up into this big meadow, an abyss of grass as far as the eye could see; it had no end and no beginning. *Where was this place?*

"Come on," he said, "this way."

I followed close behind, thinking   Hourglass would never run out of food or water—he could die here happy.

A minute later, I looked up to see a cabin tucked away in a small opening of the trees on the far west side of the meadow. *It's a beautiful little house, but this is*

The meadow was incredible, the grass was almost waist high for us and belly high for the horses. It was even hard to make them walk- they just wanted to eat. I finally gave up, pulled the tack off Hourglass and let him go; he wasn't going anywhere. My only problem would be catching him later.

Diablo had an ease to his saunter, his gait almost God-like. He turned to gaze at me following, then stepped up on the porch of the old cabin. I followed reluctantly, unsure of his demeanor; something was different. The place looked vacant, but yet in perfect condition.

On the porch were two brand new chairs, set up to show prestige. It was like walking into the mercantile in town. As though the cabin had just been built, everything was perfect. There were no marks, no wear, nothing. Diablo's ease and calm state of mind today did nothing for my sanity. The only thing I felt was the knot in the pit of my stomach.

I watched in slow motion as Diablo reached for the doorknob. It was excruciating waiting for him to open the door. *Oh... come on.*

I could feel my heart pounding, the sweat beaded under my palm wrapped around the handle of my gun. The intense anxiety made it hard to breathe. I just stared at the handle; *please hurry and open the door!* A few seconds felt like a lifetime.

I felt the blood rush from my head, and dizziness filled my body. It was difficult to stand; my legs were failing. I fought to breathe. My vision blurred, and everything went black.

"Boy…. are you alive? Boy??"

The sound resonated in my ears but I could not speak. A few seconds later, a large hand flattened against my face. I jumped to my feet grabbing for my gun. *What?*

Diablo grabbed my shirt and kept me from falling off the porch, "What's wrong with you?" he shouted.

"I… uuuhhh, never mind. Go ahead, ignore me." Diablo shook his head at my actions. I just wanted to move on and pretend this never happened.

Diablo unlocked the door and flung it open, then stepped back for me to see the interior. I stood in the doorway, completely flabbergasted at the sight. How could this be possible? Where in the world…

Diablo stood at the edge of the door frame, as a bellboy would when entering a hotel.

"Well come on, let's go!" he said.

I just nodded, there were no words uttered. Diablo swung the door closed and it felt like my freedom evacuated the premises. It was the second time today that an overwhelming force left me immobile. The cabin was filled to the brim with everything you could imagine. My soul ran for the hills that day, and I would not see it again for many years.

The past vanished as if I was washed from the face of the earth. My head screamed for answers, I had a hard time comprehending anything at that moment. I could see Diablo's mouth moving, but there was no sound. The last thing I remember was sitting in a chair listening to Diablo talk about this cabin. However, none of his words registered. When my vision finally cleared, I was riding Hourglass toward home with no recollection of what transpired in that cabin.

The events in my life from that moment forward took control and I became the passenger of a speeding train on a collision course. My universe consisted of an unending realm that created chaos across the countryside.

I spent one more night at my father's ranch before we left the next day. As I saddled Hourglass that morning, the doubts vanished. Any sense of joy from this place had vanished, and I knew it was time to move on. I bid the place goodbye and walked away from the past. But, as I have learned, no one runs from the past. It eventually comes back and smacks you in the face when least expected.

Diablo wanted to meet at dawn, he said we had a long ride to our destination. So, the bunch arrived just after sunrise, in a valley about a hundred miles from the middle of nowhere. The business owner was looking to hire some security while transporting a load of nitro south to a crew building a section of the railroad.

The job had us traveling through some very dangerous territory; not only did the Indians want you dead, but raiders were looking to hijack the cargo. Nonetheless, it paid well, and there were no marshals to enforce the laws in these parts.

As we made our way across the territory, we rode through several small towns picking up other men Diablo hired for the job. My head was filled with uncertainty as to how I'd fit in with the bunch. On a few occasions, I hunted with my father, but he never trusted me enough to use a weapon, let alone a pistol, and never shot anyone.

There ended up being seven men total in the crew, and the next morning the details of our jobs were laid out by the owner of the company. My job was riding on the buckboard, assisting the driver when necessary. Traveling with such volatile cargo meant dangerous times ahead. Needless to say, I felt like a fish out of water.

The crew had a one-point man who was the tracker; he knew the safest route. Then in the back of the wagon were two men. One drove the team and the other watched to make sure the bottles stayed upright. If they started rocking around too bad, we all went boom. The other men rode shotgun, watching for unsuspecting marauders. I played gopher: go for this and go for that. It suited me fine, I was not about to argue with anyone.

Each bottle was packed in a small wooden box filled with straw for a cushion. The boxes were designed specially to fit snugly against the frame. A black swing was situated under the cargo to allow for jarring; it kept the boxes from sitting directly on the wooden bed.

They said the trip would take two weeks; each man carried two days' worth of rations on his horse. The rest was loaded in packs on Hourglass, and we could pick up more along the way if necessary.

I was instructed that night to leave any hesitation, laziness, or fear behind. None of this nonsense would be tolerated. I knew that meant a shot in the head and my body left for the vultures.

At that moment, my future looked grim at best, and that was if I survived the job. The only shining light was my horse grazing in the yonder pasture. Somehow, his presence grounded the small part of me that still existed.

Before the crack of dawn, I felt a kick against my boot. "Get up boy, time to head out."

It was pitch black, only the stars to light our way. In the distance, my horse was standing idle in the tall grass. The mark on his forehead made him hard to miss. The wagon horses were already hooked up and ready to move. I tied off Hourglass to the back of the buckboard and jumped in the wagon, eager to be done with this job.

The first couple of days went off without a hitch until we hit uncivilized land and the terrain got bad, to say the least. A good day's travel might be four miles. Many of the hills were so steep and rough, we had to unhook the horses and carry the bottles by hand to the top, or spend part of a day clearing brush just to get over the hillside. I thought farm work made your hands bleed; by the end of the first week, they just were bloody stumps. My gloves had more holes than my hands.

I ate last, cooked when necessary, fed and watered the stock, basically did every menial chore you could imagine. When I got to sleep, it was on the hard ground with every rock, cactus, and bug to poke you, stick you, or bite you. However, when sheer exhaustion takes over, any place to lie down is heaven on earth.

We finally made our destination intact: no injuries, shootings, or deaths. Diablo patted my back, and said, "Job well-done kid, you'll make it yet." It felt good to hear someone pay me a compliment. He sent me to the livery stable with the horses and when I came back, he had my pay.

I was tickled at the idea of getting paid for my hard work. At least someone appreciated determination. "Go get yourself a room and bath, see ya in the morning," he stated.

The weight of the coins in the red bag surprised me. He wasn't going to get any arguments from me. So, I checked into the motel and ordered a hot bath, but admittedly the curiosity was killing me.

The bellhop took my bags to the room, and got me a few extra towels, while they drew my bath.

"Thank you. Come get me when the bath is ready," I said to the bellhop.

"Yes, sir," he replied. It was cool to have someone call me sir.

I grabbed my gear and headed upstairs, but the higher I got the more my pace slowed. Out on the range, you don't notice how much your body starts to ache. Which made the staircase grow as I climbed the steps.

My gear dropped just inside the door, and I collapsed on the bed. A mattress never felt so good, however, no amount of pain was going to stop me from counting my pay. Although, I admit no amount of wages may be worth this pain. I dumped the coins on the bed next to me and began to count. *5.... 10......! There is 15.00 dollars in this bag.* My preoccupation with counting my money passed the time, and the next thing I remembered, the bellhop was pounding on the door, telling me it was time to check out. After admiring the shiny coins on the bed, I had fallen asleep and woken up twelve hours later from the pounding.

"Yeah, just a minute," I hollered. When my feet hit the floor, I almost fell. Thank goodness, the bedpost was within reaching distance. *Ohhh… my father worked me hard, but this was a whole new pain.* "Is my bath ready?" I asked.

"No, sir," he said. "That was last night and you never came down."

"What!" I hollered. "What time is it?"

"Almost two o'clock, sir."

"Yeah, alright, tell the desk clerk I'll stay another day, run me a bath and I'll come down to pay."

"Yes, sir. But you will have to pay for a second bath as well. And you have a message waiting at the front desk," he stated.

"Yea, fine…. I don't care. I'll be right down, thank you," I yelled out.

I limped to the door and pulled on my boots; nothing seemed to be working this afternoon. It was frustrating trying to figure out who would have left me a message. Diablo knew I'd be at the hotel. The stiffness hit me about halfway down the stairs when I realized my money was lying in the middle of the bed. *Oh, please don't steal my money….*

The money from Diablo would be more than I'd ever see in my lifetime, but the agony of the jobs was much more than I ever expected. *Maybe I need to walk away while I still can.*

The desk clerk handed me the bill and sent the bellhop off to ready my bath. "Can I get you anything else, sir?" he asked.

"No… but I was told there is a message?"

"Oh, yes certainly." He handed me a note.

"Jed: Had to take care of some unfinished business, be back in town tonight. There is a gift waiting for you at the mercantile. Pick the one you want; I have already paid. Be ready to leave at dawn, we are heading out for the next job. You did great work; the trip went smoothly with all your help. Giving you a chance to prove yourself was worth the effort. Someday you will be an invaluable member of my crew. See ya in the morning, Diablo."

My life had come to a crossroads. One direction would have saved me from me, and the other forfeited my soul. I should have run anywhere but straight ahead. Hourglass and I should have headed for home and suffered through living on my father's ranch. But an unyielding force kept drawing me in deeper until I passed the point of no return.

The message cleared my suspicions, and I was able to convince myself it was the ignorance of adolescence—it was the pain and soreness in my body making me cranky.

"Sir, can you hold my bath for a few minutes? I need to run an errand," I asked the desk clerk.

"Sure, let us know when you are ready." I nodded and headed for the mercantile.

It was a wonderful cool afternoon; a soft crispness filled the air. My brain went into high gear conjuring justifications for my decision to stay on with Diablo.

The store clerk knew just who I was when I entered the mercantile. "Come on in, Jed. Your package is right over here in this last case. I just need you to tell me which one suits you best," he stated enthusiastically. *What in the world could be so all fire important?*

The afternoon sun glistened on some polished objects displayed in the last case. It was a familiar image, one that sent chills up my spine. Diablo's favorite pearl-handled Colt 45.

"Jed, I believe this one is yours? Diablo ordered it with your name carved in the barrel. Now, there are several types of gun belts you can choose from."

He took the pistol out of the case and laid it on the counter in front of me, and I just stared at the pearl handle. "Are you sure this is mine?" I asked.

"You are Jed, aren't you?" he said.

"Yes, I am."

"Well, Mr. Diablo is a special customer. He even wanted a rush on having your name carved - I had it done this morning. The gun belts are right over there, just pick what you like. The bill has been paid."

The moment I strapped on the gun belt and holstered my pistol, every bit of Jed disappeared; he was no longer just a menacing distraction. My rage became the controller of every decision I made for the next fifteen years. My craving for supremacy quickly grew into an addiction where dominance clouded all judgment.

I chose a smaller gun belt so there was a full view of the pistol and no one would question my intentions when I walked into a room. My understanding of control began to feel comfortable. It became apparent why Diablo grew fond of the habit. Once I walked out into the city street with a gun attached to my hip, the overwhelming notion to carry the pistol in my hand was exhilarating. It was like calfskin, how it just formed right in the palm of my hand. It felt good. The gift was an incredible action on Diablo's part – it sucked me right in for life.

The fascination of my new toy took any focus off the people in town; while I enveloped the thrill, a group of rabble-rousers grabbed a young woman and tried to drag her out of the saloon. I reacted instantly, without any thought for my safety, "Hey," I hollered out, "What do you think you are doing?"

"Mind your own business, boy, now go on, get out of here," one man said.

"I don't think so! Now let her go," I yelled.

"Or what, you'll run get your mommy?" he answered sarcastically.

"I mean it. Let her go!"

"Come on then, boy. Make me, make me," he demanded.

The man had drug the woman down the alley and slammed her head against the wall; then he motioned for me to make him stop hurting the girl. I followed close behind and the fistfight commenced after I entered the alley. Shortly thereafter, another man joined in and jumped me from behind; he forced me on the ground while both men took turns punching me. Amid the tussle, I was able to grab my gun without suspicions. It felt good to stick the pistol in my assailant's side. After threatening to shoot him, both men backed off and left us alone.

My injuries, while not life-threatening, left me badly wounded. It was difficult to regain my bearings. The young woman grabbed my arm and helped me back to the motel. She left me in the lobby and went to get the doctor while the desk clerk had the bellhop carry me upstairs to my room.

The next thing I remembered was seeing the young girl sitting in the chair next to my bed. "Where am I? And who are you? I gotta get outta here," I stated in agony.

"Hey, now lie down, you can't go anywhere for a while," she said.

"But, but I…."

"The doctor will be back this afternoon to check on you again," she replied.

"I have to go; my boss he's waiting for me," I exclaimed.

"Relax, he was here this morning. Rest. He'll be back in a few weeks to get you. I told him what happened and he left this note for ya," she stated.

"Jed: Doc told me what happened and I'll be back in a few weeks. Not to worry, the girl you saved is alive, thanks to you. Diablo."

I spent the next several days in and out of consciousness from my injuries. The woman I saved, Annie, would bring me supper each night on her way home from the saloon. She unknowingly gained my trust in a short time - it was one step in the right direction.

It was almost two weeks before I was able to get up and move around - I nearly died from pure boredom. Diablo returned a few days later fired up and ready to head out, so Doc wrapped up my ribs and gave me some medicine for the pain. I was told to take it easy for a few more weeks to let my ribs heal. The ability to ride with broken ribs is an understatement, to say the least. So, I was basically useless, and couldn't even saddle my own horse.

The quarter milers had the speed, but were not always a smooth ride. However, Hourglass seemed to know I was hurt; he went for weeks with no hump in his back until my ribs healed.

We rode outright that afternoon for places unknown. Diablo was extremely secretive about our next job. It took the better part of three days to hit our destination, and sleeping on the hard ground was excruciating. There was an unusual air in Diablo's manner. He kept silent the entire trip, except for barking out orders. I could not figure out if my situation had him perturbed or if it was just the next job.

We traveled with the usual complement of seven men, but since he supplied me with a weapon this time, I assumed the appointment must be serious.

After the third day, we made our destination, a small town just north of the border. Diablo knew these parts incredibly well, so it was obvious he had grown up here or at least spent some time in this area.

We did not check into the motel. Instead, we stayed in a small cabin outside the town limits. Only two men were allowed to leave at a time, I was escorted by Diablo personally. As he explained, I was the newbie and he didn't want me to be alone. Nonetheless, suspicions had me questioning his statement.

After we returned from supper and buying supplies, he finally informed us about our next job. I sat and listened intently at the details of the employment contract. My impression left me to believe I was the only one sitting on the outside looking in. Everyone else sat and fiddled with their guns and talked amongst themselves. Supposedly, we were escorting a Wells

Fargo stage carrying payroll across the border to an Army outpost in the middle of nowhere. However, the trek would take us across one bad section of Mexico. It was a prime target for heists due to the remote location. The reason for secrecy was apparent now, but it didn't ease my concern.

Diablo said the drivers were the only ones who knew each day's schedule. There would be fresh horses for the stage waiting at each checkpoint along with food and supplies.

It took three days of travel to hit the Mexican border. Diablo alerted everyone to be on their toes. We were told to shoot first and ask questions later; if one of us hesitated and did not do our job, we'd be shot and they meant dead. Somehow, I knew that wasn't a joke.

Later that evening when most of the crew settled in after dinner, Diablo was alone back by the chuck wagon and I knew it was my chance to speak with him about my apprehensions. It was the second time his response sent chills up my spine. I swallowed hard and went to my bedroll.

The next morning Diablo woke me before dawn: and said we were heading out early. I still had not recovered from our last conversation. However, if I was to survive the next day, I had to put those thoughts away permanently.

We all carried our own rations for each job and refilled about every three days. I grabbed some breakfast and got a few sips of coffee. I was the low man on the totem pole, and that meant I got the leftovers. After eating, I grabbed my gear and saddled up to head out. Hourglass was settling into his new surroundings quite well; at least that was comforting.

Diablo rode back with me that morning and explained how the next few hours would proceed. We were headed into a flat, very desolate part of the Mexican desert, and he was sure we'd hit some resistance immediately. The marauders liked to attack right at dawn; travelers lowered their defenses because the night had passed, and with the light changes it was easier to ambush their victims. Needless to say, my concerns continued to grow.

I came to the quick conclusion that if there was a God, He had forgotten I existed. At this point, I would have taken any opportunity to escape the pending situation, but none of my prayers worked. Over the next hour, the first wave of resistance hit, and luckily no one was injured. The lead riders were able to stop the oncoming posse before any of them could get to the stage. However, that was not the case with the second round, they were able to flank us from the rear. Diablo whirled and started shooting, he looked over for back-up. I knew in that instant the actual ramifications of carrying a gun. It seemed cool at first until you are faced with reality.

We immediately headed for the closest cover and in this case, it happened to be the stagecoach. The driver had turned the coach sideways, so they could shoot from either direction. I could hear the bullets whistling through the air and the sounds of men being shot. They were falling like the little yellow ducks at a shooting gallery when the fair comes to town. As soon as we got to some cover, Diablo looked at me to carry my weight. In this case, it turned out to be easier than I accepted. A few well-placed shots made it appear I was pulling my own on shooting back.

As we hunkered down trying to stay clear of the gunfire, the moment of truth smacked me in the face. One of the drivers got hit in the leg, which left one less man to guard the payroll. He struggled taking cover, which left my head screaming…. run, but my heart beckoned to take a stand. As the man crawled across under the wagon, I knew it was time to earn my wages.

He nestled in under the wagon, panting from the exhaustion. But he never gave up the fight, he kept shooting and reloading his pistol. A few seconds later, he grabbed my arm, "Kid, they need your help up there."

Of course, this is where the path meets the road, and kids turn to men. Diablo was not far away; the decision had been made - there was no turning back.

Being shot by Diablo scared me more; he'd leave you to suffer in the middle of the desert with a bleeding gut shot.

I took a deep breath and climbed inside the stage, but the next few minutes were blank. It was as though my soul ran for cover while my body remained empty, stagnate without a conscience. I'd been firing the entire fight, but not intentionally aiming for someone. My hands started shaking, and I almost back off when Diablo's face flashed out of the corner of my eye. The fear rushed throughout my body; any turning back now would lead to my death as well. I held my breath and aimed out the back of the stage at the closest gunman.

When the gunslinger saw my pistol pointed out the stage window at his head, he dashed the door. I saw the whites of his eyes widen as he knew the result. His face was scarred from a life of chaos like he knew his sins would mean an eternity in hell. *Steady… aim… fire….*

The words ran through my head over and over, until it was too late. My finger squeezed the trigger ever so slightly; the hammer pulled easy. Before I realized what happened, the man fell dead. I stared at his body lifeless and knew one day, I would be in his position. The chaos made my actions easy to justify. Diablo placed six notches on my gun belt that day, and my fate as a gunslinger stood with proud distinction.

In what seemed like a lifetime, the gunfight lasted twenty minutes. The count was four of our own and one stage driver. But Diablo's actions once again came as a complete surprise. He insisted we dig graves for the men, build a cross and give them last rights. As we gathered, Diablo pulled an old black leather bible from his saddlebag, and I almost fell over. We stood listening to the short sermon baffled by the vision wearing an all-black duster

The next couple of days went along without a hitch. We all agreed it was a blessing if any were being delivered. I was assigned to ride up top with the driver.

After being shot in the leg, he couldn't handle driving the horses for more than a few hours at a time.

Diablo took the lead and we had the other two men riding on either side of the stage. Hourglass trotted along behind the stage, while I sat up top with plenty of time to think about the previous events, nonetheless, instead of feeling remorse, there was no sensation at all. I felt dead, like the men who just died by my hand.

As time passed without a conscious to control my intentions, I became relentless about adding more notches to my gun belt. It turned out to be the perfect job: a justified right to kill. Nothing mattered anymore; time didn't exist, the hours turned into days and days turned into years. There was no job too dangerous. You can't kill someone already dead — at least that is what I thought.

"Finally grow strong in the Lord, with the strength of his power. Put on the full armour of God so as to be able to resist the devil's tactics. For it is not against human enemies that we have to struggle, but against the principalities and the ruling forces who are masters of the darkness in the world, the spirits of evil in the heavens." **Ephesians 6: 10, 13**

The Rage

The unrelenting life of a gunslinger yielded untold violence. After such time, a calm overtakes the soul that envelopes the body. One day runs into the next with no intermission, no matter how much the mind craves an outlet. In the brief moments of rest, seeking the comforts of a madame, a bottle of whiskey, and sometimes a poker game can relieve the restlessness even for one night.

We'd been working one job after another for months. Diablo's obsession with money was unimaginable. Finally, when a break appeared between contracts, the crew headed for the nearest town. In a fit of certain defiance, I joined a poker game in the local saloon. It was the one forbidden act Diablo enforced on the crew. The risk of a confrontation was too great.

He always said, "A well-fed man is not desperate and won't make stupid mistakes."

I had become a valuable member of the crew and learned how to manipulate Diablo. As a matter of fact, most of the men never lasted very long anyway, so it made my presence invaluable. Besides, it didn't matter what he thought of my decision; the worst he could do was kill me, and really, I was already dead.

I sat at the bar, watching some of the locals play poker at a table in the saloon. I'd overseen so many of my father's games it was one of the only things I ever learned from him. After a few hands, a chair opened up, and it was time to try my hand at the card game.

The other players did not know I'd been watching their tells for the last half-hour; it gave me a huge advantage. Over the next few hours, I cleaned out every one of their money; except one player, and he was intent on winning at any cost. His plan, however, failed, and I won the next several hands. Since he had no more money and no one else had the cash to continue the game, it allowed me to leave. I'd never been one anyway to endure crowds for too long.

Besides, sooner or later, someone was going to recognize me and want to settle a grudge. Nonetheless, the man did not share my opinion to leave. The scene brought the bar to a screeching halt, as he regaled me with his insults about cheating and such. It had little effect since I didn't care about his issues. His insults continued as I strolled out the doors, which included his vow for revenge. They were nothing I had not heard many times before.

The sounds of the bustling saloon resumed after I exited the establishment, which slowly faded as I made my way down the boardwalk. A calm I hadn't experienced in quite some time consumed my body. It wrapped me in a cocoon of entitlement, one that suited my stature in the world. As I meditated over the emotion, a sudden jolt interrupted my reveling when a sharp pain brought me to my knees.

A few seconds later in my groggy frame of mind, someone dragged me into the alley. In my state of confusion, fighting my captor was impossible. He stuck a gun between my ribs, grasping my arm, and insisted I kept quiet. I reluctantly went along with his nudging. It was apparent the man from the saloon was making good on his word. By all rights, he had the upper hand. I had let my guard down leaving the saloon, and he took advantage, something any good gunslinger would have done. The incident gave proof of Diablo's adamant rule about no gambling.

My mind swirled, trying to gather some strength while the man struggled to drag me down the alley. I was no longer that skinny little kid my father left to survive alone on the ranch. It was the first time anyone had ever been able to jump me from behind.

Diablo's words rang loud and clear, "Lack of awareness will get you killed." I could see him glaring at me with those black pools of evil, just daring me to smart off with a sarcastic response. It irritated me most of the time, because he was never wrong, ever.

When we hit the middle of the alley, situated in the dark and out of view of the street, the man reached for my sidearm. The action brought me to consciousness; it was enough to threaten my life, but taking action was a different story. We wrestled as he continued to grab for my pistol; the struggle brought me out of my stupor. When the scuffle paused, it gave me time to look up at my attacker. Only it was not whom I expected, and the man from the bar had not hunted me down to complete his threats. His face looked familiar; I'd seen him before, or he was at least a relative. The shock of his identity made me lose my advantage, and the man snatched my gun.

I heard the pistol slam against the wall behind me, and my rage emerged uncontrollably. If this was the end of my life it would not be without a fight. The seething anger coursed through every fiber of my being, and all the years of pent-up hatred came forth. Any conscious thought vanished as I lunged toward the man. A loud thud echoed throughout the alley when we slammed against the building on the opposite side of the alley.

The thrust brought reality to a head, as terror quickly covered his face. Since my initial days with Diablo, I'd watched countless men die but this time was different, it was close and personal. I enjoyed every thrust, the punches hit hard and solid. After a few minutes, I forgot the target was a human. It was as though my consciousness had vacated the premises and pure evil invaded my body. As the punches intensified, so did my purpose. I became judge, jury, and executioner.

The relentless attack lasted one punch after another until total exhaustion took over and I collapsed on the ground next to the corpse. Tranquility settled the rage as he gasped his last breath. The fight soothed the malevolence coursing through my veins, and my body succumbed to peace.

As I mulled over the situation reality crept in, slowly forcing clarity. The kind of awareness that rushes through your body with a vengeance. My presence in the alley may have been noticed by a passerby to witness the horrific scene. A sense of urgency forced my immediate departure from the alley, and I made a hasty passage to the hotel.

It was unclear how long I had been with the man in the alley, but it was time to make myself scarce quickly. As I reached the edge of the alley, another thought rushed through my head: my clothes must be covered in blood, and entering the hotel in my present attire would be difficult. *Unless the desk clerk had retired for the night.* It was a risk I would have to take. I stopped at the edge of the building and listened for anyone talking or moving around. When all was quiet, I made my way down the boardwalk and hoped to secretly keep out of sight. My plan worked perfectly until I entered the hotel and realized my pistol was still lying in the alley next to a dead man. A gut-wrenching notion came to mind as I remembered the carving in the handle. It would be a direct path to the hanging gallows. The yearnings that drove me in town to let off some steam vanished instantaneously. It would be a miracle if my presence remained anonymous in this situation.

I took a deep breath and headed back to the scene of the crime, but the farther I walked the quicker the images of my fate raced through my mind. Nonetheless, it was a chore that had to be completed. I moved swiftly without attracting attention as I entered the alley. The darkness was a welcome cover to conceal my presence.

When I entered the alley, an eerie silence filled the air; my actions stared me square in the face. The reason for this man's conduct would forever remain a mystery. So, there was no way to justify my behavior. I'd never faced such a predicament. It was easy to kill someone in a gunfight, but without knowing his intentions, this incident would haunt me forever.

I struggled through the next few minutes, grabbing my gun and racing out of the alley, and up the stairs to my hotel room. My heart was pounding so loud I couldn't hear any sounds around me. I just wanted this night to be over and to never repeat such an experience.

The door slammed behind me, and I disappeared into the safety of my room.

The streetlights illuminated the room well enough for me to light the lantern. However, the light brought a terrifying sight. I had used my undershirt to wrap around my hands while I darted to the room, but the image that appeared before my eyes brought reality to a new level. The clear freshwater that filled the bowl was deep red; between the blood of my victim and the oozing sores on my knuckles, no amount of water was going to ever wash the stain away.

I tore my shirt into strips and wrapped my bleeding hands to help stop the agony. *If I could only wash away the rest of the night.* An uncontrollable exhaustion consumed my body, and I fell back on the bed, and within seconds I was in a deep slumber. In my unconscious state, fatigue stayed in control until the wee hours of the morning.

As the night hours waned, my unconscious state began to wear off, I felt moist air blowing on my face as if someone was standing over me. Their heaving breaths pressed against my ears, and I awoke in a cold sweat. But as I struggled to open my eyes and protect myself against this person, it was a useless battle. I was held captive in my nightmare. Their breathing grew stronger every minute as I fought to escape the hideous dream. The cold sweat turned to uncontrollable shaking; I could not stop the terror from invading my mind.

Finally, I broke free from the restraints only to find an even more terrifying sight. I screamed, "You're dead; I killed you, I killed you. What are you doing in my room?"

His cold dead eyes stared at me with an intense odium of evil. *What do you want from me*? I saw every nuance of his face, each line in his forehead, the two-day stubble, and empty sockets that once had a soul alive and breathing. Just as I was witnessing this unending incubus, the vision played repeatedly. By now, I'd scrambled up the bed, forcing my shoulders against the headboard. As I inched my way up the wall, the vision matched my moves precisely. There was no escaping this hallucination, I started screaming, "You're dead, I killed you." As panic forced my shrieking, a voice from the hallway called out, "Mr. Jed is everything, all right? Are you okay?"

I couldn't move; nothing was working. I just stood screaming, "Stop! Stop! Go away." I had to make the visions stop.

While I fought to free myself, a hand roughly grabbed my arm. The space was pitch black, and there was no way to locate the person struggling to pull me down. Then… I felt a cold chill overtake the scene, and the appearance of a large hole formed beneath me. I could hear the air swirling, moving under my feet. I fought with every ounce of strength to gain freedom, but I couldn't stop my descent into this abyss.

My arms flailed about, reaching to clutch anything within my grasp… nonetheless, the descent continued. I pleaded, "Stop! Stop! Please make it stop!"

Then all of a sudden, everything came to an abrupt halt, and silence ensued. I lay there gasping for breath; my body froze. The blackness enveloped everything; there was no light anywhere. *What… where am I?*

In the silence, the thumping in my chest echoed through my head. It pounded as if I had just run ten miles from an angry bull. I knew this had to be real or was it?

An uncomfortable light filtered throughout the room and allowed me to see and scan my surroundings. I had escaped the confines of the bed, but an image in the mirror brought reality to ahead. I was no longer dreaming; the nightmare was real.

I saw deep pools of evil staring back at me, there was no mistaking the physical evidence. My deepest fears had come true: my essence of innocence was forever gone. The torn pieces of my shirt were soaked in dried blood, and it completely covered my arms and hands. My face had bloody handprints christening my cheeks. *Oh my God… what have I done?*

A red veil enveloped the room. It had to come off, *please get it off!* The basin turned red, but my hands remained the same color. I pleaded to cleanse myself of this nightmare.

When the water stopped working, I grabbed the towel and wiped my arms dry. *This is a dream; it's not real; get ahold of yourself.* I sat down on the bed to catch my breath and think for a moment. I had to settle down. |That man attacked me, what did I have to worry about? I was only protecting myself. It was time to relax and get on with my day, forget about last night; it was just a bad dream.

The pep talk worked for the meantime; I was able to regain control. After a short time, I grabbed my clothes and headed downstairs to take a hot bath and shave; I just knew that's what I needed. Then a good hot meal and I'd be back to my old self, ready to go to work.

I spent the next several minutes regaining some composure and cleaning my hands of the blood. Since no trace of my actions needed to be seen by the public.

Once my heart calmed, I grabbed a clean shirt and headed downstairs, "Good morning, Mr. Jed. Is everything all right?" I shuddered.

"Yes, yes, why do you ask," I asked.

"We just heard some commotion coming from your room last night," he said.

"Oh, that! Just a bad dream, nothing to worry about; everything is all right." The comment was more to reassure me than the desk clerk.

"All right, sir- here is your towel." I nodded, knowing he did not believe my explanation. *What if they heard me screaming, or worse, what if they heard the words?*

I continued to pursue the self-talk, as I needed time to think. My story had to fit the incident. The only option was to walk down the alley and examine the scene. Diablo would say, do not admit to anything unless there is evidence to prove the accusation. We had been on the trail for quite some time; maybe I just needed to take a vacation. *You know cowboys get that trail fever after being out for a long time.*

My plan worked: a shave and shower did the trick, and I felt like a new man. I would go get some breakfast and forget the whole incident. *I'll just take a walk on this beautiful sunny morning.* I was still trying to convince myself.

My brain went into overdrive, concocting a strategy as I headed down the boardwalk toward the saloon. Finally, a solution hit me: I would stop in front of the alley and check my boot for a rock or something. It would give me time to inspect the alley.

I slowly scanned the street for any passersby before commencing my plan. Once I pretended to flinch from a pain in my foot, I stepped off the boardwalk and took off my boot. The alley just happened to be right next to me. Although, the sight brought an alarming but calming sensation. The alley was empty; nothing, no sign of anything. It was as ordinary as any other day.

My thoughts quickly jumped to the conclusion that I drank too much whiskey while playing poker.

The relief felt good; it appeared the wretchedness I feared hadn't ruined my soul. Since morning cleared up the previous night's reveling, I decided to take Hourglass for a ride. It had been a long time since we just rode for fun. Maybe I'd even take a fishing pole, and head for the creek to camp out under the stars for a few days. I had not fished since, leaving my father's farm. A calm peaceful setting away from town was just what the doctor ordered. *A great idea!*

I paid my tab at the hotel and headed for the livery stable to saddle up Hourglass. Once my saddlebags were packed with supplies it was time for a three-day vacation. Our next job wasn't scheduled until Saturday. Diablo would be at the hotel restaurant for breakfast. *Some time to myself...*

I returned at first light Saturday, rested from a wonderful fishing trip. By the time I refreshed my supplies, Diablo was already at the restaurant. We exchanged pleasantries during our meal but kept business details until we hit the trail. However, he appeared quite sober this morning; something had him distracted.

The meeting with our client was a few hours from town, but Diablo remained silent for the whole ride. On most jobs, he always filled me in on the way but this time was different, and it had me a bit nervous about his passive demeanor.

Once we finished with the client, Diablo informed me we would be heading back to town; he needed to refill his supplies. My calm peace of mind vanished instantly. Of course, he knew nothing of the incident, but hiding anything from Diablo was next to impossible. However, in this case, the distraction might be a blessing. We headed to the mercantile, which directed us past the alley that may have been the scene of a horrible crime. I swallowed hard and dug deep into the stirrups. Just when I thought this nightmare was over it haunted me once again.

We hit the livery stable and noticed three guys carrying shovels, which usually meant someone had died. The undertaker stayed busy most of the time. Nonetheless, the coffins remained empty outside the mortician's office. *What?*

I nearly crawled out of my skin when Diablo spoke up: "Well another body is hitting the dirt." He turned and looked at me, "What's wrong with you?"

I contemplated for a few seconds, "Yep, I see that, but the coffins are empty?"

"Those are new ones waiting for the next victim. I saw them carrying the dead guy out back when I came into town earlier. He's in the wagon waiting on the preacher." Diablo's words stopped time; I couldn't breathe. My vision blurred and nothing made sense. "Let's go for fun and pay our respects." It was an unfortunate game we played, seeing how many of our enemies died before us.

What... I screamed silently. The gut-wrenching fear returned. I had to do something to alter this course of action. Then a voice of rage dared me: *Come on… what's the matter? Are you scared? He attacked first, remember; you were only protecting yourself. Only a coward would shy away from seeing the face of his enemy.*

Amid my internal fight, I unconsciously followed Diablo over to the wagon. "Hey, do you know him, kid?"

I paused…. choking back the words, "No- no… I've never seen him before."

"You didn't even look," he exclaimed.

My decision had been made, the option to ride away disappeared. *This day is never going to end.* I prayed for my vision to fail. Nonetheless, karma smacked me square in the face. I couldn't look away, his cold dead eyes tried to pierce my soul. It drew me in deep like I'd never seen a dead body.

"Hey, kid, are you there? It's like you've never seen a dead body. What's the matter with you?"

"Yeah, I'm here. Let's go get outta here." I was never so glad to leave a town.

"Are you getting soft on me?" he asked.

"No way man, are you kidding? I love this shit." At that moment, nothing was further from the truth. It was hours before we had any conversation. The idea of recapping the scene was unbearable. Our next job was a great distraction.

Of all the days to have a routine patrol. It took maybe an hour to settle in and get the layout. Then we were back to silence; not even Hourglass would pitch, he just walked along with the dead quiet. *Oh… dead; bad choice of words…* I begged for a wolf, bear, or rattlesnake, anything to kill the calm. Our job lasted almost a month and the pay was more than we'd make in six months, but it was nothing but silence. The time passed without a single disturbance. I found myself egging on any man trying to instigate a fight, although nothing could muzzle the incessant quiet. The next best solution came when we hit the bar on our first break.

My colleagues took a bath and hit the restaurant for a steak, and I chose the local saloon. I grabbed a drink at the bar and surveyed the room for any women suitable for an evening of fun. After my selection was made, I bought another drink and asked the bartender to deliver it to the lady at the end of the bar.

As she turned to see who sent the drink, I tipped my hat. She nodded, and I accepted. *Now I'd get some action.* A few minutes later, her acquaintance demanded I let go of his woman. Of course, I declined. We exchanged a few words and he insisted we go outside and settle this matter. The entire bar followed us to the street. I was prepped for a knockdown drag-out fight, instead, he pulled a gun. In seconds, the barrel of his gun was pointed directly at my forehead. The same rage took over before I had a chance to think and his gun was on the ground. Only in this case, there was a huge audience. I felt the cold dead hand of death grab my arm and struggle to pull me into that hole again. I started screaming, "You're dead, I killed you, you are dead."

The crowd's commotion stopped immediately after my outburst. Then a few minutes later, I heard a familiar sound; the sheriff had come to arrest the participants. "Come on kid, you are coming with me tonight to sober up in a jail cell."

Gratefully, I had enough sense to calmly go with the sheriff. The night would give me time to regain some sense of sanity. "I'll cut you loose in the morning, but I better not catch you in my town again. Understand?" I just nodded my head.It was about 8 o'clock when he let me out, and I knew Diablo would have my head. At least the incident would break the silence. Between being gone all night and in jail, the lashing was extreme. He had every right to chastise my behavior; it was inexcusable. It was most likely the worst lashing I had ever taken, one that made my father look like a saint. It would be the last and final time I ever made that mistake again.

For the next several months, the visions in my head settled down and things went back to normal, so to speak. Diablo finally calmed down and forgave my mistake, which was not soon enough. I saw many of his rampages; however, they were never directed at me.

Although my actions created a major event in camp, it was not the main reason for Diablo's rage. While I took my time off to relax and fish, Diablo learned a bounty hunter was gunning for him. In most cases, he just ignored the claims, but this time was different. It stirred him up, and my spending a night in jail exasperated the situation. We had been together long enough for the authorities to connect us. It was likely they'd shoot first and ask questions later; dead or alive did not matter on the bounty.

"Jesus looked at them and said, 'How hard is it for those who have riches to make their way into the kingdom of God! Yes, is easier for a camel to pass through the eye of a needle than for someone rich to enter the kingdom of God.' Those who were listening said, 'In that case, who can be saved?' 'Things that are possible by human resources, are possible by God'." **Luke 18: 24.**

The Overview

As youth fades, maturity forces clarity on the decisions of your past. It has a strange way of drawing your attention to reality. A few weeks back, we had an altercation with some raiders, and one of the men looked very familiar, although I could not place from where. When the situation settled down, I asked Diablo, and he gave me some bullshit about his identity. Then he scooted around the question by ordering me to get back to work. His reaction caught me off guard; I'd never known him to lie about anything.

The following night during Screwball's watch, while the rest of us slept we were attacked by a gang of ruthless bounty hunters. Amid our battle, I caught a glimpse of Diablo sneaking out of camp, leaving the rest of us to defend ourselves. It was the first time I had ever seen him split in the middle of a fight. One of the first rules when I agreed to ride with Diablo was to never leave a man behind. The choice to leave us hanging left me bitter. Of course, we hunkered down and fought through the war. The raiders gave up after a short time. A few hours later, Diablo wandered back into camp as if nothing had happened. When I called him out, he glared at me and walked away. Our time together gave me insight into when to leave him alone. Needless to say, my suspicious rose as to why he showed up after the gunfight ended. The next morning, he gave me some lame excuse about seeing a man standing on the edge of the tree line. By the time he got to him, the chase was on, although he lost him in a thicket of trees.

Since there was no evidence to prove otherwise, the truth must remain untold. Although, his reaction to seeing the bounty hunter a few weeks back left me seriously doubting the explanation. Diablo never minced words; I always considered him as a friend, and he'd share anything with me. But in this case, something was awry.

My suspicions continued to rise over the next few months. Diablo finally after all these years begin to show its true colors. He proved to be a man with many faces.

The job went off without a hitch, and we headed out for the next gig. After setting up camp, Diablo left to meet with our new client. In most cases, he'd ask for me to join him, although today I was told to stay in camp. A few hours later, he returned with some news that I found highly unsettling. We were heading for my old stomping grounds. I had not been home in over fifteen years. The information left me speechless.

I could not even remember the last time my father crossed my mind. Nevertheless, it left me wondering if the old house and farm were still standing. As the shock wore off, I found a strange sense of joy filtering throughout my body. *My, how time changes people.*

As the week wore on, utter delight sank in deep; I was anxious to see the old farm. Plus, it had been years since I'd said hello to Mom. Diablo's preoccupation kept him from noticing my elation, for which I was grateful. The peace was welcome.

Diablo kept most of the job details to himself, except that we were escorting several ammo wagons to the Army outpost along the far southern border. It took us across the same territory as my first job with Diablo. Most of the gigs we took were of this nature, however, something was seriously wrong. I tried several times over the last week to discuss my feelings but was disregarded each time. The only reply was something along the lines of me being a coward. It was a moot point, which made my decision to leave this crew much easier.

Our job started in just over a week, which gave me a few days at home to check out the homestead. The possibility of starting a new life seemed appealing. It is funny how things were coming full circle.

After supper that evening, I informed Diablo of my plans for the next few days. Since he was completely preoccupied with this job, it had little effect on his attitude. It didn't bother me anyway; I needed a break. At first light, Hourglass and I headed for home. We cut off on the back-road home. Once we turned at the old sawmill, the memories flooded in like a rushing waterfall.

I remembered when Hourglass was a two-year-old, racing down this small path for the first time. The sensation caught me so off guard I stopped and walked to the farm. As we walked along stargazing, it was amazing how little things had changed. Other than the size of the trees, it all looked the same. Dad used to come along with the buckboard every few months and trim the trees - we used the wood in our fireplace. It was obvious no one had been at the homestead for quite some time. The lane was so narrow I had to duck a few times.

It felt like Christmas when I was a kid, waiting until morning when Mom would have saved enough money through the year to buy me one small gift. It would be wrapped in plain brown paper, tied with a string. The memories brought an unrecognized smile. *Ohhh…man.*

The old house was still standing in relatively good condition. *Dad would be… may be dead by now. Wow…have I been gone that long?*

"Come on, Hourglass, let's check out the house," I told him. He shot over to the green grass behind the house. I felt a strange rush of emotions reaching for the doorknob. I remembered the last time… *leave it alone!* I left, vowing to end his life if we ever saw each other again. The time away has yet, again altered my reality.

The door stuck, as it always had. It used to upset my mother, and she'd pleaded with dad to fix it; he'd always shrug her off and go about his way. I shoved the door with my shoulder, and it burst open. It was the same; nothing had changed. *What happened? It's been empty all these years?*

A sense of peace I never expected rushed through my body. It felt good. I needed to find some answers, but first, one important stop had to be made. Our family cemetery sat across the pasture on top of the hill. It was a long walk, but I needed the exercise. Hourglass was head-first in the pasture grass, he wasn't going anywhere.

As I crossed the pasture, my emotions welled deep, nothing made sense. *What had I done?* My unimaginable lifestyle wreaked havoc on my mental state. I had spent years hating this place and for what? All the money in the world cannot bring happiness: a feeling that was quickly brought to my attention.

The cemetery was in a deplorable state, however, my eyes focused on one headstone newer than the rest. Once I managed to pry the gate open, I got a closer look at the name. It was Dad. But, the date… he died the same month I left home. All these years I carried a grudge for a man that was already dead.

I needed to solve this mystery. It was time to head for town and talk with the county recorder's office. Diablo would forbid the action, but it was time for a change. I had listened to him all my life; he no longer controlled my every thought. After gathering up Hourglass we enjoyed our ride to town. I wanted to enjoy the day. Nothing seemed more pressing than feeling the warm sun against my face.

As we rode through town it looked small, I always imagined it bigger. The only change was the new church at the edge of town. We stopped outside the recorder's office. I knew the old man would not recognize me, I had a few gray hairs now and some age on my face. "Yes sir," he said. "What can I help you with?"

"Can we sit down? This might take a bit to explain. My father was Jacob Foster, and the old farm is still empty. Can you tell me the story? I already went to the cemetery and saw his grave."

"Say that again? You are Jed Foster?" he said, astonished.

"Yes sir, I am. I have been gone for a long time and thought it was time to come home. Is the old farm for sale? Can I buy it?"

"Buy it! Your father left it to you lock stock and barrel when he died. The place has been empty since he passed. We take the money for land taxes out of the account he had. However, there was no money to pay last year's taxes and the place goes up for auction next month," he replied.

"How much are they? I'll pay you right now, sir." I said. "But can we keep this quiet for right now?"

"Yes sir, Jed. Yes sir," he stated.

"Where do I find the records of my father's death?"

"Well, the file is right here. Although, I need you to go down to the lawyer's office and sign a copy of the will, so I can release them to you."

"I will be right back. Thank you." The idea of legal issues never came to mind when I signed the papers.

A short time later I returned to the office with the documents he requested, signed and notarized, "I'll leave you alone to read the information."

My reading skills were subpar since my schooling stopped shortly after Mom died. Dad never saw the sense of going to school. Since the legal stuff did not make sense, I skipped straight to the death explanation. Seems my father was shot by a man while playing poker in the saloon at the other end of town. The man was never caught; the only information known to the marshal was the shooter went by the alias Diablo.

"Make a tree sound and its fruit will be sound; make a tree rotten and its fruit will be rotten. For the tree can be told by its fruit. You brood of vipers; how can your speech be good when you are evil? For words flow out of what fills your heart. Good people draw good things from their store of goodness; bad people draw bad things from their store of badness. So, I tell you this, that for every unfounded word people utter they will answer on Judgment Day, since it is by your words you will be justified, and by your words condemned."

Matthew 12: 33, 37

Finding Un-cleanliness

I realized one thing that day: Running from your past will never solve any problems. I mulled over the words in that document on the ride back to the farm. *How could I have been so wrong about my father?*

As I rode up the long path behind the barn, Diablo was waiting on the front porch. His presence was not completely unexpected, but I had to find out what he knew about my disappearance. "What are you doing here?" I asked.

"Where should I be?" he blurted out.

"I don't know, you have been very distracted lately. I had no idea what was going on with you."

"I had business to attend to."

"Well, I had business as well. What did you expect? I have not been home in fifteen years."

"Are you pulling that card with me? I know you better than you know yourself."

"I went to town, there was someone I wanted to see."

"So, you are telling me this was not the first place you came?"

"No, I was just back through here after my business." My heart pounded, lying to Diablo was not smart. I only hoped he believed my story.

"Well since we are here, let's take a look. Then we can head back to camp. You won't get lonely!" He was suspicious but bought the explanation.

It took everything I had to keep quiet about the new information. A man I trusted for most of my life killed my father. He may have been rough on me, and even brutal at times, but that did not give Diablo the right to shoot him and then lie to me all these years.

The ugly truth of Diablo's guilt showed itself over the next few days. He suddenly became my best buddy. It also explained his reservation about taking the new job. As truth played its hand, my value became crystal clear. As a gunslinger the one lesson I learned was patience; everyone makes a mistake sooner or later. My time with this group had come to an end. I just had to figure out a plan, as leaving Diablo would be dangerous. I guess my prayer had been answered; a few days ago, I was asking for some action to break the silence, but now I was praying for quiet to think.

The pressure of staying in one place for too long was eating Diablo alive. I'd never seen him so anxious, although his anxiety gave me some peace. He just kept asking if I had any business in town to take care of before he headed out in the morning. It got so bad one of the other guys said, "Man, what's the matter with you, the kid said "no" several times."

"I just can't believe you don't want to see the marshal and ask about your father's death."

"How do you know my father is dead, Diablo?" I asked.

"Well he was an old man, and it's been a long time since you left."

"I don't need to see the marshal for those answers, everything would be at the lawyer's office. Besides, why should I care? All he ever did was beat me. Nevertheless, going to the marshal is against your orders. Right?"

"I am sure we could make an exception; I'd want answers." The crew was starting to take note of his radical behavior and ask questions as to his motives.

"Yu, a, got some bad deal with the kid?" Screwball asked. "Why u so furred up with him goin' to town and seein' the marshal?"

In an instant, Diablo got mad, threw his hands in the air, and walked off. The crew stood staring at each other with their jaws on the ground at his antics. We didn't see him for the rest of the night.

I spent most of the evening staring at the stars. My mind was riddled with questions. We headed out at the first light for the loading docks. Diablo never said a word the rest of the job, unless it pertained to work. The silence, in this case, was a blessing. It gave me the time to think and make some very important decisions.

I knew the job was going to take quite some time, especially traveling south with several buckboards loaded with that much ammo. I had to act fast to set my plan in motion.

It would take a few hours to load all the wagons, so I made my way to the outhouse. Although, I ended up at the one behind the mercantile. Diablo would be watching my every move, so I paid a young kid to take my papers to the marshal's office. One had the signed documents, and the other was a message. The information was the coordinates of our route to the Mexican border. Now, all I had to do was let fate play its hand. My intentions had to remain secret.

I calmly rushed back before anyone noticed my absence. However, I admit for the first time in my life, doing the right thing felt good, no matter the consequences. A gunfighter learns quickly; circumstances can change at a moment's notice, so you must always be prepared.

On one job we had several years ago, a gunfight broke out leaving us pinned down for hours. During the battle, a buddy sitting next to me, covering the other side of the window, got distracted for a few minutes when he stopped to reload his gun. As he looked up to start shooting again, a bullet came through the window, hitting him in the forehead. It was the first time I saw a colleague die nearby. I can still feel the blood as it splattered on my face.

Diablo saw the event and hollered, "Kid! Get your head on straight. I can't afford to lose another man; you can worry about him later." At the time, I thought it was because he cared about me, but in reality, I was just another expendable body that he needed to complete the job.

Our crew shrank and grew with each passing day when a man was killed, and he just went and found more. I'd been lucky up to this point, but that could change at any time. I knew a change was coming, and I accepted it with open arms. At least dying would relieve me of the rage I lived with daily.

The upcoming days proved Diablo remained in the dark as to my plan. I tried to stay clear, hoping he would not get suspicious. Although it was not just staying quiet, my behavior had to appear normal. If I had learned one thing over the years, Diablo could read people like a book. It was a trait that kept us alive during many encounters with other gunslingers. I had a feeling of relief to be ending this lifestyle and the present time seemed appropriate. The news about my father was just the icing on the cake; once the veil had been removed the lawless acts I had been a part of were an unavoidable issue. It has been said you can't ever go back; however, when the present is bleak, what other choice do you have? I could either stay with Diablo and die out on some prairie left to rot while the vultures picked my bones clean or go home and pick up the pieces.

Nonetheless, the change was a blessing in disguise… if I survived.

My guard was on high alert, waiting for the right moment to escape. Our caravan moved across a pasture bordered on the north by a densely forested section. As we closed in on the area, I waited for my chance to escape. A few seconds later, one of the lead wagons hit a pothole, causing the cargo to shift. The perfect distraction gave me the chance to slip out through the woods. Once I hit the shadows, Hourglass hit full throttle; we had to put as much ground between me and the crew as possible.

Hourglass carried himself with perfection, it was as though he knew the severity of our situation. Before long, we were in unfamiliar territory, and it was time to trust my horse. The riders would be following quickly behind us, and we had to keep going. I kept a close eye on Hourglass for signs of exhaustion, but he seemed resistant to the pressure. The trail opened up into another large pasture with a creek running along the south side. We took up a spot in the shadows and gave my horse a break where he had time to drink and rest. I knew we had about thirty minutes before the group would be on us.

Once we broke free of the thicket, Hourglass was rested and ready to run. We had to keep pressing for safety. The terrain had opened up into a vacant desert expanse. I started to worry about Hourglass; he had been running hard for quite some time. Our situation brought on a reflection about my life, and what I had accomplished. Diablo's world had no beginning or end to the chaos. All the dreams I had as a kid were gone as if that part of my life vanished the day I left home. At least my father had built something: a farm, a family, and some wealth. Granted he was brutal and I always felt like he hated me, but he had something to show for the fruits of his labor. At that point, I realized, my vision of reality was warped. I never took the time to understand what my father felt about losing Mom. Instead, I was wrapped up in my own grief. It's obvious there was little to no communication between us. *Maybe it's time to face the reality of my sins and repent.*

In my dazed confusion, the sun peeked over the distant horizon. It seemed my prayer had been answered. I found myself in this wasteland of despair with no memory of the previous events. The glaring rays made it hard to see across the glinting grains of sand. I tried to shake off the stupor, however, it seemed determined to keep me hostage. *Where am I?*

As the sun continued to rise, I could feel the heat burning my skin and I searched for my hat. My hand patted the ground behind me, but instead, it touched something unconscionable. My heart stopped; the thought brought terror flooding through my body. *Hourglass… What have I done?*

The agony overtook my soul and left me paralyzed in the hot desert sand. I would for once in my life take responsibility for my actions. Reality mocked my pain as I scooped one hat full of sand at a time. My vision blurred with the streaming tears, dropping one by one on the lifeless body laying silent. The longer I dug, the rage spilled and left me screaming, "It should be me lying there! I am the one who should be dead, not him!"

I shouted until my voice quietened, leaving only the sounds of my thoughts racing in my head. I wanted to die right alongside my horse.

By the time his body was covered, the exhaustion settled deep, leaving me on my knees begging for guidance. *How could redemption be granted after what I have done?*

The sun glared across the sand. It was blinding and forced me to look down at the horrific reality of my actions. Then, lying there between my knees facing the heavens above… was the salvation I had been looking to find all these years. In the process of burying the one being in my life that brought hope to end the chaos, was my mother's cross. I hated her for leaving me all those years ago, yet somehow, she knew that one day, I would need salvation from God.

The End

"Do not let your hearts be troubled. You trust in God, trust also in me. In my Father's house, there are many places to live in; otherwise, I would have told you, I am going now to prepare a place for you, and after I have gone and prepared you a place, I shall return to take you myself, so that you may be with me where I am."

John 14

Author Bio

Anna provides it all as if you are in the saddle along for the journey. Her rare books bring the readers joy from nearly every genre they can appreciate. She exuberantly brings the image and sentiments of the West to full life throughout the storyline. Yet, at the core of Judd's work is a black stallion who engages life in every aspect of the book. Haystack fills children's minds with wonder as he interacts with Marshal Spur and the Outrider Gang, to the mild-minored young steed who brings Adam to new levels of learning in his life. Then he is brilliantly portrayed as a beautiful Appaloosa stallion in the Broncobuster as Cash.

Anna is one of the greatest novelists and a freelance ghostwriter who is known for equestrian professionalism in every genre. Her young adult fiction novels and all books bring joy to the readers.

Faith and Works

"What good is it, my brothers, if someone says he has faith but does not have works? Can that faith save him? If a brother or sister has nothing to wear and has no food for the day, and one of you says to them, 'Go in peace, keep warm, and eat well,' but you do not give them the necessities of the body, what good is it? So also, faith of itself, if it does not work, is dead. Indeed, someone might say, 'You have faith and I have works.' Demonstrate your faith to me without works, and I will demonstrate my faith to you with my works. You believe that God is one. You do well. Even the demons believe and tremble. Do you want proof, you ignoramus, that faith without works is useless? Was not Abraham our father justified by works when he offered his son Isaac upon the altar? You see that faith was active along with his works, and faith was completed by the works. Thus, the scripture was fulfilled that says, 'Abraham believed God and it was credited to him as righteousness,' and he was called 'the friend of God.' 'See how a person if justified by works and not faith alone. And in the same was, was not Rahab the harlot also justified by works when she welcomed the messengers and sent them out by a different route? For just as a body without spirit is dead, so also faith without works is dead." James 3; 14:26